SAM DOWLING
Is a Dublin-born playwright. He has written and produced nearly thirty plays or small-cast versions of classics for Praxis Theatre Laboratory. His subject-matter has ranged from Irish history through the lives of writers and artists to re-working of themes from the Greek myths. His play about the Brontës (co-written with Andrea Bird) has had three productions in Tokyo.
For more detail see listing in playwrights' database at
www.doollee.com

PRAXIS THEATRE LABORATORY is an experimental theatre which seeks its direction from the actors' response to the work. No-one takes on a separate role as director. We particularly value images conjured in rehearsal, and intuitive and emotional rather than intellectual or technical evaluation. We try to fix as little as possible and each performance retains an element of improvisation.
Founded by Sam Dowling as the in-house company at The Tabard in West London from 1984, in 1990 we left to pursue more experimental goals. We opened a small theatre space in County Roscommon, Ireland in 1999 and have toured UK, USA, Ireland, Belgium, Netherlands, Ukraine and Poland.

This small-cast version of THE CHERRY ORCHARD [for seven actors] was first performed at Boyle Arts Festival, County Roscommon in 1997 with a cast that included;
OLIVIA .... Maria Straw
GAY .... Sam Dowling
VERA .... Maggie Gallagher
PETER TIMMS .... Michael Appourchaux

For production permission and terms, contact Sam Dowling.

IRISH PLAYS AND OTHERS BY SAM DOWLING
IN PRINT AT WWW.LULU.COM OR IN THE PIPELINE

RIVERMAN [Walter Greaves, naïf painter, rise and fall.]
CAULDRON OF BRONTËS [Genius siblings.]
A SEASON IN HELL [Wild poets Rimbaud and Verlaine.]
MOUNTAIN [Life-changing encounters]
RENEWAL [Site-specific version of MOUNTAIN]
TROJAN WOMEN
BIRTH OF THE BEAST [Northern Ireland.]
BIG FELLA! [Michael Collins.]
ALLEGIANCE [IRA in London.]
ANTIGONE
THE FLAME AND THE STONE [Yeats and Maud Gonne.]
VIRGIN OF NOTTING HILL [Sexual problems.]
ORESTEIAN TRILOGY
LOVELOST [Abuse]
RED COUNTESS GREEN CROW [Markievicz and O'Casey]
HA! HA! HA! [Improvisations on Coward and Shakespeare.]
CHARTISTS RISING [London 1848]

AND SMALL-CAST VERSIONS OF THESE CLASSICS;

THE CENCI
IMPORTANCE OF BEING EARNEST
CHERRY ORCHARD
THREE SISTERS
HEDDA GABLER
WHEN WE DEAD AWAKEN
HAMLET
MACBETH
ANTONY AND CLEOPATRA
THE TEMPEST

IRISH PLAYS AND OTHERS: Volume 12

CHEKHOV'S
THE CHERRY ORCHARD

in a new version by Sam Dowling
set in Ireland in the 1970s

e-mail praxis.lab@ntlworld.com

Published by Lulu 2008

www.lulu.com

© Sam Dowling 1997

All rights reserved

ISBN 978-1-84799-507-0

THE CHERRY ORCHARD

THIS VERSION of THE CHERRY ORCHARD IS SET IN IRELAND in 1970s

DRAMATIS PERSONNAE

OLIVIA RANELAGH......................Lady of the Manor House

GAY..Her brother

VERA..Her adopted daughter

ALEX O'PARK..Businessman

PETER TIMMS...A chronic student

DINEEN..A maid

ASHBY..A manservant

PART ONE

> [Early Spring. The cherry trees
> are in bloom but the ground is white
> ... with fallen blossoms or frost ?]

O'PARK
That's it. The night train

DINEEN
It's day light already

O'PARK
That train is late
(Yawns) I really wanted to be there to meet them
Sat down and dropped off... Why didn't you wake me ?

DINEEN
I thought you'd gone
I hear a car

O'PARK
......? No

DINEEN
Can you imagine ? Five years ?

O'PARK
I wonder has she changed
She was so....natural
I remember.... I was only a lad of maybe fifteen
We were in the yard out there delivering stuff
My father, God rest him, had been drinking
We had the hardware shop then
He punched me right on the nose for some reason...
When he was drinking, you know...?
I was pumping blood and she saw me and took me in

I never saw such a beautiful young woman...
Little more than a girl herself
'Don't cry little peasant,' she said
'it'll be better before you're twice married!'
....
Little peasant...
That's what my father's people were I suppose
Small farmers we'd say
And here I am now eh?
Still a bit of a bull in a china-shop maybe
'You can take the man out of the bog
But you can't take the bog out of the man'
Except I could buy and sell the lot of them
....
Been reading this book... fell asleep

DINEEN
The dogs barked all night
They know

O'PARK
Are you all right, Dineen?

DINEEN
I'm shaking
I think I'm going to faint

O'PARK
A little too ladylike for your own good
Your hair... everything
You don't look like a maid

DINEEN
The gardener brought the flowers in
I'll do them now

O'PARK
Get me a gin and tonic first
Like a decent girl

DINEEN
Yes...sir
...
Mr O'Park... I have to tell someone
You know Joe McArdle your bookkeeper ?
He's proposed to me

O'PARK
Yes ?

DINEEN
I don't know what to do

O'PARK
That lad is not the full shilling

DINEEN
I don't know what to do
I like him quite a lot
And he says he's madly in love with me
He's sort-of accident prone

O'PARK
Don't I know it
We call him Catch 22

DINEEN
I was wondering... is... is his job secure ?

O'PARK
They're coming !

DINEEN
Oh God ! Oh ! I.....
I'm all hot and cold !

O'PARK
It's them all right !
Come on !
Will she recognise me after five years ?

DINEEN
I'm going to faint !

> [They exit and return at once with OLIVIA,
> VERA, GAY and ASHBY, who carries luggage.]

VERA
My hands are numb with the cold

OLIVIA
> [She will shed a lot of joyful tears.]

I loved this room. 'The nursery !'
I used to sleep here as a child
Oh Gay ! [Kisses him]
I feel like a little girl again
Oh Vera ! [Kisses her, then him again.]
And Vera never changes
You look like a nun, dear !
And I recognise Dineen [Kisses her]

VERA
Your rooms are just as you left them, Mother dear
The white and the mauve

> [Exit all except DINEEN and GAY.]

GAY
That train is never on time

What a way to run a railway !
....
So, I have returned with the prodigal mother

DINEEN
It was snowing when you went for her
And now the cherry trees are in bloom
Oh I have to tell you
Mr O'Park's book-keeper proposed to me while you were in France

GAY
I haven't slept for two nights
Chilled to the bone

DINEEN
I don't know what to think

GAY
Is that frost under the cherry trees ?

DINEEN
He loves me so very much

[Enter VERA.]

VERA
Coffee for Mother, Dineen !

DINEEN
I won't be one minute

[She goes.]

VERA
How was Paris then ?

GAY
I found her living in a fourth floor flat
Pretty scruffy
The place was full of all kinds of strange people
When she saw me, she looked so sad

She cried and cried, I thought she'd never stop
Just hung on to me and cried and...

VERA
Don't go on, please Gay, don't

GAY
She had nothing
And neither had I
We barely scraped up enough for her fare home
And of course, she kept ordering expensive meals
And tipping all round her like there was no tomorrow
And insisted on bringing that Ashby fellow home.
We can't afford a manservant:
He expects to eat just as we do

VERA
I never liked him

GAY
Well, what's new ? Have you paid the interest ?

VERA
What do you think ?

GAY
Oh dear

VERA
The estate is up for sale in August

GAY
Oh dear !

[O'PARK sticks his head into the room
and bleats before disappearing]

O'PARK
Baaaaah !

VERA
Oh I could murder that man !

GAY
Vera... is there any news on that front ?
                    [She shakes her head.]
He loves you
What are you waiting for ?

VERA
He thinks about nothing but work
I wish I'd never met him now
I can't stand the sight of him
The dogs in the street yap on about us
We'll never get married
It's all unreal, like a bad dream

GAY
I went up the Eiffel Tower

VERA
All day... around the house...
All day I dream and dream...
If I could get mother settled down
My mind would be at rest
I might go on a kind of pilgrimage
To all the beautiful and holy places
Just from one to another... on and on...
Wonderful !

                              [DINEEN enters.]

GAY
The birds are singing in the cherry orchard

VERA
It's not worth going to bed now

> [VERA and GAY leave.
> ASHBY enters: he tries to
> speak in a posh accent.]

ASHBY
May I go through here ?

DINEEN
Ashby ! I hardly recognised you

ASHBY
Oh yes ? And who are you, may I ask ?

DINEEN
Dineen... McDermot. I was only... that high, when you went away
You wouldn't remember me

ASHBY
Oh wouldn't I ?
Juicy bit of fruit I'd call you

> [A quick look around and he
> grabs her: she utters a little squeal.
> Enter VERA.]

VERA
What's going on ?

DINEEN
I tripped and nearly fell
He caught me

VERA
A trip is for luck

                                        [Exit ASHBY.]

DINEEN
I could do with it
Should I tell Madame that Peter Timms is here ?

VERA
He's asleep
I put him in the wash-house
He doesn't want to intrude

DINEEN
He was your teacher ?

VERA
My little brother's tutor. Gerald
He was drowned

DINEEN
I remember, God rest his soul
That's why Madame ran away, isn't it
She couldn't bear it
Oh it makes me so sad

VERA
He was only seven

DINEEN
Why did Peter come here to bring it all back ?

VERA
He......
                    [Enter OLIVIA with GAY and O'PARK.
              GAY mimes playing billiards, as he is wont to do.
                                        DINEEN will leave.]

OLIVIA
How's this it goes ?

'Pot the red in the corner
Double into the middle pocket.'

GAY
'And straight into the corner !'
Remember when we slept in this room, Olivia ?
And suddenly I am quite middle-aged

O'PARK
Aye time flies

GAY
Pardon ?

O'PARK
'Time flies' I said

GAY
This place stinks of mothballs

VERA
Well, gentlemen
Mother needs her beauty sleep

OLIVIA
You're always mothering me, Vera. [Kisses her]
I'll have that coffee and then we'll all go
I drink it day and night

VERA
Is all the luggage in ? [She goes to check.]

OLIVIA
Is this really me sitting here ? Ha ha ha !
I want to jump around like a... [Buries her face in hands.]
Say it's all a dream ?
God, I love this country of mine ! I love it so much

In the train I couldn't look out for crying...

O'PARK
I have to leave for London in an hour or two
I want to just sit here and look at you
Talk to you

GAY
It's the Parisian clothes

O'PARK
This brother of yours thinks I'm a thick
A penny-pinching peasant
I don't mind, Mrs Ranelagh... Olivia
So long as you believe in me as you used to
With those wonderful eyes
Good God in Heaven !
You are magnificent as you ever were
My old man used to empty your family privvy
For a few coppers from your grandfather
But you and only you did so much for me
That I forgot all that
That I love you as my own flesh and blood
More than my own flesh and blood

OLIVIA
I can't sit still; I can't   [She will pace about frantically.]
This happiness is too much to bear !
Laugh if you want. I'm such a fool
My darling bookcase, I kiss you
My sweetest table, I love you !

GAY
You know that Nanny died while you were in France ?

OLIVIA
Yes, I know

GAY
And Aggie... and one-eyed Michael left to join the police...the Guards.

[GAY has a habit of taking out a box
of fruit drops or something and popping them.]

O'PARK
I have good news to tell you [Looks at watch.]
I must be off in a moment
As you know, your cherry orchard is being sold to pay your debts
The twenty-second of August. But not to worry
Lose no sleep, there's a way out, my dear
I have a plan, so listen
Your estate is well placed near the road and railway
All we do is
Break up the cherry orchard into plots
Ditto the land with river frontage
Understand ? Building sites to let or sell
Problem solved. Q.O.D.

GAY
Rubbish !

OLIVIA
I don't understand the logic, Mr O'Park

O'PARK
They'll sell like hot-cakes
Sold out by Autumn or I'll eat my hat
Boating and swimming in the river
This old house must go, of course
I'd say good riddance
And the cherry orchard had its day
Three generations back

GAY
You're talking through your backside, dear man

The cherry orchard is sacrosanct
Nothing like it in the county

O'PARK
It's very big
You haven't sold a cherry for ten years
The crop itself is hit and miss
And mostly miss

OLIVIA
The orchard is mentioned in an encyclopaedia

O'PARK
I have to go
If we don't do something your entire estate
Will go to auction on the twenty-second of August
Take my word there is no way but my scenario
There just ain't no other way

GAY
There was a cherry factory here in Grandpa's time
We had a recipe
Sent them all over the Empire

O'PARK
What recipe ?

OLIVIA
It's lost

O'PARK
The country's changed
Ordinary folk have cash to spend
On holidays and leisure
Work from home
That class is growing fast
Your cherry orchard has a future

For a thriving happy people

GAY
Rubbish
We know the land and people

[Enter ASHBY.]

ASHBY
Two telegrams, Ma'am

OLIVIA
They are from Paris

[She tears them up without reading them.]

I've finished with all that

GAY
Do you know, Olivia, how old this bookcase is ?
The date is carved at the bottom: 1798
Can you imagine ?
Perhaps some revolutionary built it for our ancestors
We supported the United Irishmen you know
Mustn't let them forget that up in Dublin, eh ?
An inanimate object, but still... a bookcase !
....
Venerable bookcase, I salute you !
For how many generations you have devoted yourself
To the highest ideals of goodness and justice
For how many generations have you filled us
With an urge to useful work
For how many generations have you sustained
Our courage and our faith in a better future
With your silent call: you have fostered in us
The ideal of public good and social consciousness.... eh....

OLIVIA
You never change, dear Gay

GAY
Eh... I pot into the corner pocket !
I pot into the middle pocket !

O'PARK
It's time I hit the road

ASHBY
Would you care to take your pills now, ma'am ?

GAY
Don't do it !
Let me have them

[He empties the pills into his hand, blows on them, and swallows the lot with a glass of water.]

OLIVIA
You're mad !

GAY
I've taken the lot !

O'PARK
What a digestion ! [ALL laugh.]
I'll see you in three weeks' time

[Kisses OLIVIA's hand: shakes ASHBY's.]

Au revoir, Gay
I really don't want to go
Olivia, you'll think about the building sites and let me know, won't you ?
I can get a very big loan on that score
Give it serious thought

VERA
I thought you had to go

O'PARK
I'm going, I'm going   [He exits.]

GAY
What an ignoramus !
Sorry ! Vera's going to marry him: he's Vera's beloved *fiancé*

VERA
Enough is enough, Uncle Gay

OLIVIA
Well, Vera, I for one will be glad. He's a good man

GAY
I say, can any of you lend me two hundred and fifty quid ?
I have to make a payment on a loan tomorrow

VERA
We haven't got it: really we haven't got it

OLIVIA
It's true. I have nothing

GAY
Never mind. Something will turn up
Sometimes I'm in the blackest despair
Utterly ruined... all lost ! And lo and behold something happens !
Quite out of the blue
I think I'll buy a sweepstake ticket

VERA
The sun has risen, it's warmer already
Look, Mamma dear, how beautiful the trees are !
My God ! The air here is wonderful !
I never heard so many birds singing !

GAY
The orchard is all white
You haven't forgotten, Olivia ?
How straight our long avenue is: straight as a die
Like a ribbon that's been stretched tight
It shines like silver on a moonlit night. Remember ?
You haven't forgotten ?

OLIVIA
Oh my childhood, my innocent childhood !
I used to sleep here in this nursery
I used to look out at the orchard from here
And I woke up happy every morning.
In those days, the orchard was just like that
As it is now, nothing has changed. Ha ha ha !
All, all is white ! Oh my orchard !
After the wild stormy autumn
And the dark cold winter
You are young and full of joy again
The angels have not forsaken you !
If only this burden could be taken from me !
If only I could forget my past !

GAY
Yes
Now the orchard is going to be sold to pay our debts
Strange

OLIVIA
Look ! There's Mother, walking through the orchard
In a white dress. It's her !

GAY
Where ?

VERA
Poor Mama !

OLIVIA
It's no one. Imagination.
See over there to the right
Near the summer-house... a small white tree
Bending over...like a woman

                                              [Enter TIMMS.]

TIMMS
Mrs Ranelagh.... I'll just say hello and...
I was told to wait till morning but I...

VERA
This is Peter Timms

TIMMS
Peter Timms. I used to be Gerald's tutor...
Have I changed so much ?

OLIVIA
......   [Puts her arms around him and weeps silently.]

GAY
Now, Olivia !

VERA
I told you to wait, Peter [She is weeping too.]

OLIVIA
My Gerald... my little boy.... Gerald... my son

VERA
Mamma love... God took him back

TIMMS
Don't... please don't

OLIVIA
Drowned.. Why would God want him drowned ? Why ?
Why did God want him, my friend ?
Forgive me... ranting and raving like this
....
Well, Peter, what has happened to you ?
You were such a beautiful young man

TIMMS
Heh. I heard a woman on the train call me 'moth-eaten'

OLIVIA
In those days you were a bit of a lad, weren't you?
Are you losing your hair ?
You were a typical student then...

TIMMS
I'm a chronic student as they say
It is a terminal condition. Heh.

OLIVIA
Well, off to bed with you now

     [Kisses GAY and then VERA.]

GAY
You won't forget that two hundred and fifty
I need to borrow, will you ?

OLIVIA
I have no money, my dear

GAY
I'll pay you back without fail

OLIVIA
......

Very well then, Vera will give it to you
Give him two hundred and fifty pounds, Vera

VERA
Yes, Mother
Absolutely anything he wants

OLIVIA
Hew needs it, or he wouldn't ask

                  [Exit OLIVIA and then TIMMS.]

VERA
It's disgusting

GAY
Ughh. You smell of the kitchens young man

ASHBY
You haven't changed... sir

VERA
Your mother has been sitting in the Servants' Hall
Since yesterday, waiting to see you

ASHBY
Why can't she leave me alone ?

VERA
You should be ashamed of yourself

ASHBY
Why couldn't she leave it till tomorrow ? [Exit.]

VERA
Mamma hasn't changed either
She simply gives everything away

GAY
Y'know when you hear of lots of cures for a disease
It means it's incurable
I've been racking my brains
And I came up with all kinds of solutions...
Which means there isn't one
Someone could leave us a fortune...
Or we could marry you off to someone rotten rich
Or we could send one of you
To give the old Countess a go
She doesn't know what to do with her money

VERA
If only God would do something for us

GAY
Stop snivelling
The Countess is very rich but she doesn't like us
Firstly because your mother married beneath her
And then she hasn't exactly led an exemplary life
She is good and generous and loving...
But no one could accuse her of being virtuous
You only have to look at her

VERA
How can you say such things about my mother ?
About your own sister ?
Why do you talk so much ?

GAY
Yes... yes, you're right of course. It's dreadful
God ! And that speech about the bookcase
I knew it but couldn't stop

VERA
Just keep quiet. Quiet

GAY
[Kisses her.] I will. Quiet
But I must tell you this
I was talking to this barrister chap
And from what he says it should be possible
To get, you know, finance
To keep up the interest payments

VERA
If only God would do something for us

GAY
I'll have another chat with him on Tuesday
Do stop weeping, Vera !
Your mother is going to have a talk with O'Park:
He'll never refuse her, I'm sure
And you can go to London and see our grandmother
The Countess
We'll have a three-pronged attack and... That's it !
We'll pay the interest, I'm sure of it
            [Feeds a sweet into his mouth.]
I swear on my honour as a gentleman
Or on anything you like
The estate will not be sold ! Here's my hand on it
Call me a damned liar
If I allow the auction to take place
I swear on my immortal soul !

VERA
You're starting up again, Uncle Gay

GAY
I mean it. I....

VERA
You had better just keep quiet, Uncle dear

GAY
You think I'm a fool
I have my convictions and I have suffered for them, I can tell you
All my life
The tenants love me
You have to know the tenants: you have to know how they think...

VERA
Will you be quiet !
....   [Distant music heard.]
Did you hear bells ?

GAY
In off the cushion. Pot the white
                                [TIMMS watching VERA.]

TIMMS
Oh Vera...Vera... my Morning Star !

PART TWO

> [On the terrace. Near sunset. Beyond the cherry orchard is a large town, in the distance. Nearer we might see a dilapidated shrine, gravestones, a well. VERA and TIMMS: he carries a guitar.]

TIMMS
So we're both orphans. Brought up by strangers

VERA
Mamma gave me plenty of love
In her chaotic way
Of course she was obsessed with Gerald
Her own flesh and blood

TIMMS
Thank God I wasn't looking after him the day he...

VERA
Don't talk about it

TIMMS
If we don't talk about it
It will never be over and done with

VERA
Mamma doesn't want it over and done with
Please don't mention it again

TIMMS
I...
Well, if that's what you want
.....
Am I allowed to talk about us ?

VERA
No. Play your guitar

TIMMS
Maybe I will and maybe
I'll simply put an end to the entire fiasco

VERA
Play [He does.]

TIMMS
I always carry a revolver, y'know

VERA
Don't be silly

> [He stops playing to show her his
> revolver, then resumes.
> Enter ASHBY and DINEEN, in time to see
> the revolver. VERA moves off:
> TIMMS trailing after her, playing.]

I have work to do

DINEEN
God forbid he'll use that gun to hurt himself
I'm a complete bundle of nerves these days
Ever since I've come to work here
I've lived like a lady
I couldn't go back to the old life
Look at my hands. Did you ever see such white hands ?
Like a lady's

ASHBY
I read all kinds of extraordinary books y'know
I shall certainly be somebody quite distinguished
In a few years' time

DINEEN
If you deceive me, Ashby
I'll go completely off my head
My nerves are all on edge

ASHBY [Kiss]
You're a real peach, you are
Ay, hold on there ! I don't like girls to be too easy
It's so common

DINEEN
I love you ! Love you ! Love you !
You're the cleverest man I've ever known

ASHBY
Good God ! Don't talk that kind of filth
In my opinion girls who fall in love
Are little better than prostitutes
....
One enjoys a cigar so much in the fresh air
Oh dear ! .....? It's Madame. Get back to the house
Say you've been for a swim or something
And don't say you've been with me
It gives the wrong impression

DINEEN
That cigar has given me a headache

[Exit DINEEN.
Enter OLIVIA, GAY and O'PARK.]

O'PARK
Time marches on
A decision must be made one way the other
All I need is a 'yes' or 'no'
Will you let your land out for housing ?

OLIVIA
Who has been smoking those dreadful cigars ?

GAY
How would we ever manage without the railway ?
Imagine, we've been up in Dublin
A magnificent lunch in the Shelbourne and here we are
Back in the heart of the country !
Pot the red !
I suppose no one wants just one game...

OLIVIA
There's all the time in the world

O'PARK
One word !

GAY [Yawns.] Aaagh !

OLIVIA
Yesterday my purse was stuffed with money
And now... look !
My poor dear Vera is always trying to economise
Irish stew five times a week
And I just throw money around
Like it had gone out of fashion [Spills the contents of her purse.]
My goodness: all over the place !

ASHBY
Allow me, Madame

OLIVIA
Thank you, Ashby
Why on earth do I need to go out to lunch ?
The restaurant was full of the most awful people
And those tablecloths smelling of detergent: ugh !
Why do you have to drink so much, Gay dear ?

And talk so much ?
In the restaurant you gabbled away about nothing
The sixties and all that psychedelic rubbish
I hate you engaging the waiters
With these pointless monologues

O'PARK
Aye

GAY
I'm simply a hopeless case
What do you want ?

ASHBY
You always make me laugh, sir. I can't help it

GAY
Do I have to listen to this ?

OLIVIA
Go away Ashby. Run along like a good chap

ASHBY
Certainly, Madame. Ha ha ha ! He's a scream ! [Exit.]

O'PARK
One of the Switzers is after your land
They say he's coming to the auction himself

OLIVIA
Who told you that ?

O'PARK
I heard it in town: at the club

GAY
Our great-aunt has promised to send us money

Sometime

O'PARK
How much ? A couple of hundred thousand ?

OLIVIA
No chance. Ten or fifteen
We must be thankful for small mercies

O'PARK
I'm sorry, but you all seem to be walking in your sleep
You don't understand your position
Your estate is going to be sold !

OLIVIA
Well, what would you do ? Tell us what you'd do !

O'PARK
I tell you every day of the week !
Over and over again !
You need to let out the cherry orchard and the land for housing
And you need to do it now !
The auction is nearly on top of you !
Try to think straight !
The moment you decide to do it
You'll be able to raise enough money to save everything

OLIVIA
Housing... all those people... it's so vulgar

GAY
I couldn't agree more

O'PARK
You're driving me out of my mind !
I can't take any more of it !
You are nothing but a silly old bag !

GAY
Pardon me ?

O'PARK
You are nothing but a silly old bag !

OLIVIA
Please don't go, I beg of you !
We'll think of something

O'PARK
There's no thinking in it

OLIVIA
Please stay, I beg of you !
I always feel do much more optimistic with you here
.....
I keep expecting something to happen
As though the house might fall down on top of us

GAY
Cannon off the cushion... pot into the middle pocket

OLIVIA
The sins of our ancestors are being visited on us

O'PARK
Your sins   [GAY pops a sweet.]

GAY
The locals say I've blown my entire fortune
On fruit drops. Ha ha ha. That's impossible

OLIVIA
Oh dear: my sins...
I've always flung money around like water...
Like a woman out of her mind... I knew it

I think I even married my husband for his debts. Ha !
He died of.... champagne actually.
I am so unlucky: he was hardly in his grave
When I fell in love with another one
Quite an affair I can tell you
And just then I had my first punishment
And it nearly did for me
My son was drowned down there in the river.
Left the house, left the country
Left the river above all
Never to come back
I closed my eyes tight and ran and ran blindly
And that man followed me... without pity
Without respite... even though he was ill... really ill.
I bought a villa on the Riviera to nurse him
I couldn't leave him to die, could I ?
And for three years I knew no rest... day or night
Fighting off death with all my strength
Until it wore me out
But I cheated death out of him... God alone knows why.
I sold everything to pay our debts and went to Paris
So he could rob me again
So he could torment me again
Desert me for some tart or other
I don't know who
I tried to overdose
On something stupid and ineffectual
The shame of it ! The sin of it !
It was then that Gay arrived
I had already decided I was going back to Ireland
Back to my daughter
And yes, back to the river that had drowned my son
Oh merciful Lord God in Heaven, forgive me my sins !
Don't punish me more than I can bear !
I got another telegram from him this morning. Paris.
Imploring me... [She tears it up.]
What is that music ?

GAY
Our famous folk group
They're making quite a name for themselves these days

OLIVIA
Really ?
We must have them up to the house some evening
We could have a party

O'PARK
I don't hear anything
[Sings *sotto voce*]
   Three German officers crossed the Rhine, Haroo haroo !
   Three German officers crossed the Rhine, Haroo haroo !
   Three German officers crossed the Rhine
   To hump the women and drink the wine
   Inky pinky parleevoo !
I saw an excellent play at The Abbey last night
It was so funny !

OLIVIA
I'm quite sure it was nothing of the kind
If you would take a look at yourself
Instead of looking at plays
Your pointless empty life, your foolish conversation

O'PARK
Guilty as charged ! Ha ha ! Yes we live like idiots.
.....
My father was an ignorant tenant-farmer, a peasant.
He understood nothing and he taught me nothing
Just beat the tar out of me
Every time he got a few drinks in him
With a stick or his closed fist
I was some kind of punch-bag for him
Wouldn't let me go to school

So I'm a bit of an ignoramus
I can hardly sign my name
My handwriting is like a pig's

OLIVIA
You ought to get married my dear fellow

O'PARK
Yes, a woman might put some shape on me

GAY
You ought to marry our Vera. She's a good girl

O'PARK
Yes

OLIVIA
We adopted her you know
Her people were no better than yours
Vera knows how to work
She can work from morning to night and never rest
And she really loves you and I know
You have had your eye on her for a very long time

O'PARK
All right. I don't mind if I do
She's a nice girl
....

GAY
I've been offered a job in the bank

OLIVIA
You'd better stay right where you are

GAY
Our number was up once the British pulled out

Yet everyone seemed quite pleased about it
I suppose they had no idea what it really meant
Tomorrow I'm meeting a retired General
Who may lend us some money

O'PARK
I hope you're not depending on your General
For paying the interest

OLIVIA
There is no General
                [Enter TIMMS and VERA.]
Come here, my dearest
Oh, if you only knew how much I love you
Sit here beside me

O'PARK
Our 'chronic student' is always hanging around Vera

TIMMS
Why don't you mind your own business ?

O'PARK
He's going to go straight from being a student into being a pensioner

TIMMS
Is that supposed to be funny ?

O'PARK
What's happened your sense of humour ?

TIMMS
Get off my back, will you !

O'PARK
Tell me this and tell me no more
What do you make of me ? Honestly

TIMMS
.....
I'll tell you
You're a wealthy man
On the way to being a multi-millionaire no doubt
And to the extent that
The predators of the jungle are necessary forces of nature
Whatever function they may serve
In providing carrion for less rapacious scavengers
To that extent you too are necessary
                              [General laughter.]
VERA
You'd better tell us about life on other planets Peter

OLIVIA
No. Remember what we were discussing yesterday ?

TIMMS
I don't

GAY
Pride

TIMMS
We discussed a lot of things yesterday
But of course, reached no conclusions about anything
You may be right for all I know
That there is something godlike about the proud man
Actually it's nonsense: man is essentially flawed
So what has he to be proud about ?
To be precise, as a general rule, the Irish are uncouth
Stupid and deeply discontented
Time we stopped admiring our own reflection and did some work

GAY
Death is the leveller

TIMMS
Maybe so. But what do you mean by 'death' ?
The end of the five senses ?
Who knows but we have a hundred other senses
Ready to lead us on...

OLIVIA
I'd forgotten how clever you are, Peter

O'PARK
Oh, so had I

TIMMS
Humanity changes inexorably...
Learning, learning, creating, creating
Some day humanity will know everything there is to know
Some day humanity will control the movements of the universe
And be as God
All we, in our generation, have to do is work towards that end
And support those who seek after truth

O'PARK
His head is in the clouds

TIMMS
Most people's heads are in the sand... or muck
Wasting away their precious lives
Blind to the poverty and suffering of others
Which holds back all humanity from its destiny
....
All your long serious faces fill me with dread
All your long serious conversations fill me with despair
We should simply shut up
And do something worthwhile

O'PARK
I work a fifteen or sixteen hour day

Frankly, peasant and all that I am,
I could buy and sell the lot of you
No one has ever bested me in a deal
Because I know what makes people tick
If you want to know what people are really like
Start up a development project
You'll soon see how few people
Give an honest day's work for an honest day's pay
Sometimes I lie awake thinking about it
God has given us a country fit to breed giants
And we have populated it with pygmies

OLIVIA
Who wants giants ?
You only find giants in fairy-tales
                    [Musician seen far off, playing his guitar.]
There's one of our musicians

GAY
The sun has set, ladies and gentlemen

TIMMS
So it has

GAY
Oh wondrous Earth
Lit by this eternal light
Beautiful beyond description
Indifferent to Man's troubled fate
You whom we call Mother
Giver of life and death...

VERA
Uncle Gay: please don't start again...

TIMMS
Stuff it into the middle pocket

GAY
Sorry! Mum's the word, ay?

> [They fall silent.
> A distant sound is heard, like a
> great piano string breaking,
> resonating sadly and dying away.]

OLIVIA
What was that?

O'PARK
Don't know
A cable breaking in the mine, maybe
A long way off

VERA
A bird. A heron

TIMMS
An owl

OLIVIA
It gave me the shivers

GAY
The banshee follows this family
We heard it the night before the boy drowned

VERA
Hush

OLIVIA
My mother heard it the night the British surrendered the barracks

VERA
There's someone out there [Exit with OLIVIA.]

GAY
They didn't surrender
......
We have visitors

[Enter OLIVIA and VERA.]

OLIVIA
Well, I hadn't any change...

VERA
It was a young gypsy boy: he was quite drunk
Mama gave him a fiver !

O'PARK
That's the utter limit !

VERA
I'm leaving, I'm leaving !
The servants are expected to go hungry
And you give that waster five pounds !

OLIVIA
I am incorrigible
I can't help it
You'll lend me some more, Mr O'Park, won't you ?

O'PARK
Of course I will

OLIVIA
By the way, Vera, we've made a match for you here
Congratulations

VERA [Weeps.]
You think I'm just a joke, Mamma !

O'PARK
Get thee to a nunnery, oh Melia !

GAY
Look, I have the shakes !
Does no one want a game of billiards ?

O'PARK
Oh Melia ! My nymph: pray for me !

GAY
I've got to watch my ticker
But I can still dance with the best of them
As the saying goes, 'if you're one of the pack, wag your tail
Even if you can't bark !'   Ha ha ha !
Matter of fact, I'm as strong as a horse
My father used to say we were descended from the Romans
Well from Caligua's horse actually... the one he made a senator...
Our family motto should be
 'Live horse and they'll sell your grassland from under you'
Because we no longer have any I am obsessed with money
It's only natural
A hungry dog dreams only of meat

TIMMS
I think the horse image is more appropriate

GAY
Man's best friend
You can sell a horse
            [VERA joins them.]

TIMMS
Good evening Mrs O'Park ! Ha ha ha ! Mrs O'Park

VERA
Moth-eaten revolutionary !

TIMMS
Well, I am a moth-eaten revolutionary and proud of it
....
Gay, if your family had put into something useful
The energy they've wasted
Raising interest on their borrowings
They might have turned the world on its head

GAY
The philosopher Nietzsche
That towering intellect
Says there's nothing wrong with forging banknotes

TIMMS
You have read Nietzsche, then ?

GAY
Well, not personally
But I don't mind telling you
I'm near ready to start printing my own banknotes
The day after tomorrow I have to pay
Three hundred and fifty interest on a personal loan
I have nearly half of... My God ! It's gone ! I've lost my money !
Oh Lord, what shall I .... ?
Ah there it is ! There's a hole in my pocket
It's in the lining. Phew ! Phew !

OLIVIA
Time for supper

VERA
That gypsy frightened me
My heart is still pounding

O'PARK
I must remind you, my friends
The cherry orchard is up for auction on the 22nd

Just think about that, will you ? Think !

                        [ALL exit except TIMMS and VERA,
                                  who is drawn back by him.]

TIMMS
You and I must show them how to live ! Live with meaning
Nothing petty or illusory to stand between us and a free and happy life !
We must join the irresistible march
Towards the shining star of the new morning !

VERA
You're a bit crazy, Peter !
I don't know... things are changing all right
Even the cherry orchard seems to be changing
The trees look older and the colours less vibrant
I used to love our cherry orchard more than anything on earth

TIMMS
That entire earth is our orchard, Vera
It is wide and wonderful
Imagine the generations of labourers
Whose sweat nurtured that cherry orchard
Can you see their eyes
Looking out from the gnarled tree trunks ?
Their limbs and faces in every branch and leaf ?
Can you hear their voices ?
This family owned their very souls, Vera
Father and son for hundreds of years
That's what has made you different

VERA
I'm not really of their blood

TIMMS
Your mother and uncle and all that went before them

Fed and fattened on the souls of their labourers
Blind to a vision of the days to come
We are already living on borrowed capital
Borrowed time
Borrowed from those who dared not pass beyond the kitchen
Or the servants' hall
We know history without understanding a word of it
We have substituted conversation for comprehension
We have blinded ourselves with alcohol and self-indulgence
We cannot live in the present
Until we suffer for our past

VERA
We must suffer through unceasing labour as they did
But I want to find god too
In my own way
I will throw the keys of this house
Into the well and walk away

TIMMS
Vera, I am a young man
But already I have been to Hell
To many hells
And always I had a vision
Of a future full of happiness
I believe in that and always will

VERA
The moon is rising

[Sad music, OFF.]

VOICES
Where are you ?
Vera, where are you ?

TIMMS
Yes, the moon is rising
There !

Happiness !
Coning nearer and nearer !
                [Exit VERA.]
Vera... where are you ?

VOICES
Vera, where are you ?

PART THREE

[Lively music heard.
Dancing in the adjoining room.]

VERA
We've hired that folk group for the evening
And God alone knows how we're going to pay for it

OLIVIA [Hums to the music.]
What can be keeping Gay so late ?
Dineen, get the musicians a drink, will you

TIMMS
The auction must have been cancelled

OLIVIA
What a time to give a party ! Ah well...
I can't understand why he hasn't come home
It must be over by now
So, either the estate has been sold
Or the auction has been cancelled
Why torture us like this ?

VERA
Gay must have bought it

TIMMS
Hah !

VERA
My great-aunt sent money for it
Good will help us and Uncle Gay will buy it: I know it

OLIVIA
She sent fifteen thousand
That won't even pay the interest
My entire future is being decided today...my life...

TIMMS
Mrs O'Park!

VERA
Chronic undergraduate! They've kicked you out!

OLIVIA
Don't be so cross, Vera: he's only teasing you
Marry him if you want to....he's a nice chap
Very interesting. Or don't
Nobody's going to push you into anything

VERA
I actually take these things very seriously, Mamma dear
Frankly, I think he is very interesting. I like him

OLIVIA
Marry him then.   Stop messing about, my dear

VERA
Mother, he hasn't asked me! I can't kidnap the man
Everyone has been talking about him and me for the past two years
Everyone but him
All he does is make stupid jokes
I know how his mind works
He's making a lot of money
And all his business interests
He has no time for me
If I had the fare, I'd get on the boat tonight
And go as far away as I ever could
I'd go into a convent!

TIMMS
What a wonderful idea

VERA
One would think you'd have learned something

With all your studying !
How plain you've grown, Peter !
You are turning into a young old man before my eyes.
Oh Mama, what am I going to do ?
I must have work to do or I'll go mad

[Enter ASHBY.]

ASHBY
One of the musicians has broken a billiard cue ! Ha ha ha !

VERA
Who let them near the billiard table ? [Exit.]

OLIVIA
Don't tease her, Peter
Can't you see how unhappy she is ? She's in love

TIMMS
I am above love

OLIVIA
So, I suppose I am beneath love
...
Where on earth is Gay ?
All I want is to know one way or the other
Is it sold or is it not ? It is an utter disaster...
I don't know what to think
I want to scream ! I want to do something mad !
Help me, Peter, for God's sake ! Say something !

TIMMS
I don't give a damn about the estate
The estate is an anachronism
There is no going back to that life, Mrs Ranelagh... 'Road closed '
So, you must stop worrying: stop deceiving yourselves
Finally face up to inevitability

OLIVIA
What inevitability ?
It seems you can see inevitability and I can't
I seem to have gone blind !
You have the solution to every problem
Simply because you are still a child
And haven't had to live through the consequences of your mistakes
You look boldly into your future only because you are the blind one
And can't see what is ahead of you !
Of course, you have high ideals, and are serious and honest in every way
But do try to understand our position
And be generous... if only a little generous
Try to spare my feelings.
I was born in this house
My father and my grandfather and grandmother too
I love this house
I cannot conceive of a world without our cherry orchard
It is the centre of the world
And if it really must be sold, then sell me with it
                [She embraces TIMMS: kisses his forehead.]
Have pity on me, my dear, dear friend

TIMMS
You must know that I sympathise with all my heart

OLIVIA
But you must express yourself in a kinder way, Peter
                            [She drops a telegram,]
I feel as if I'm carrying the woes of the world on my back
You have no idea !
This place is so noisy
My very soul trembles with every sound
Yet I daren't go to my room for fear of being alone
Don't blame me, Peter.... I love you like my own son
And I would willingly let Vera marry you... honest to God !
But you have to qualify at something

You have no self-discipline...
You let yourself be tossed about by every wave
That's such a strange thing, isn't it ? Isn't it ?
Why haven't you a beard ? Have you not started shaving yet ? Ha ha !
You're a scream !

           [TIMMS picks up the telegram.]

TIMMS
I'm not interested in that kind of thing

OLIVIA
That telegram's from Paris: I get them every day
The boor is ill again, and things are going from bad to worse
He begs my forgiveness
Really, I do think I should be near him
For a while
Don't look so disapproving, Peter
He's ill, lonely and unhappy
And who's going to look after him
And make sure he takes his medicine
And doesn't make an utter fool of himself ?
And what of it if I love him ? I do, I do, I do !
And he is, he is, he is a millstone round my neck
That's pulling me down to the depths
I can't live without him
You think I'm an idiot: well, don't say it. Sssh !

TIMMS
Please... I have to say what I think
That man is robbing you !

OLIVIA
No, no, no ! I won't listen to such talk !

TIMMS
He's a bounder
And you're the only one who can't see it

He's nothing but a petty thief, a con-man a.....

OLIVIA
You are a grown man
But you behave like something out of a child's comic-book

TIMMS
Leave me out of it !

OLIVIA
You ought to be ashamed of yourself
At your age you ought to understand about love
You are not capable of love ! Of falling in love !
You're not good, you just never grew up ! You are a freak !

TIMMS
What is she saying ?

OLIVIA
'I am above love !'
You're not above love, you are emotionally crippled !
Why haven't you got a mistress at your age ?

TIMMS
Oh my God ! This is dreadful ! What is she saying ? This is dreadful...
I'm going !
      [Exit TIMMS and re-enters immediately.]

Everything is finished between us ! [Exit.]

OLIVIA
Peter wait ! I was only joking ! Peter !
      [A CRASH: TIMMS FALLING.
      Girl's laughter. Enter VERA.]

What was that ?

VERA
Peter fell down the stairs !   [Exit.]

OLIVIA
What a strange young man !   [Enter VERA with TIMMS.]
Poor Peter ! I am sorry... I was joking...
Let's go in and listen to the musicians

VERA
A man in the kitchen says the cherry orchard was sold today

OLIVIA
Sold ? To whom ?   [Enter ASHBY.]

VERA
He didn't say
Then he left

ASHBY
He was there in the kitchen, yapping away
No one knew who he was

OLIVIA
I feel something like the hand of death on me
Ashby, go and find out who bought it

ASHBY
He went off ages ago [Laughs.]

OLIVIA
I don't see what there is to laugh about

ASHBY
I just find everyone so funny these days

OLIVIA
And if the estate is sold ?

Will you find that funny too ?

ASHBY
Mrs Ranelagh
That's something I've been meaning to ask you
If you go back to Paris, please take me with you
I couldn't live here without you
It would be quite impossible
I mean, between me and you
The people here are so ignorant
No morals, no education. And it's utterly boring
The food in the kitchen is disgusting
Please ! Please take me with you !

OLIVIA
I think they want me in the drawing-room: everyone is dancing
[Exit OLIVIA. Enter DINEEN.]

DINEEN
Miss Vera told me to go in and dance
The place is full of men
I get dizzy when I dance
My heart is thumping !
Ashby, that new Post Office clerk told me something that took my breath away

ASHBY
Who let that kind off lout in here ?

DINEEN
'You are like a flower', he said

ASHBY
What ignorance !

DINEEN
'Like a flower'. I'm so sensitive...

ASHBY
It is preposterous! [Exit as VERA enters.]

DINEEN
I love when people say nice things to me

VERA
Have you no work to do?

DINEEN
You told me to go in and dance

VERA
That was three hours ago. Get back to your work
[Exit DINEEN. Laughter from OFF.]
Who is that in the Billiard Room?
[VERA rushes out: crashes into O'PARK entering.]

O'PARK
Thank you very much!

VERA
I am so sorry

O'PARK
A lovely welcome, I must say

VERA
I didn't hurt you, did I?

O'PARK
Minor concussion, I should think [Enter OLIVIA.]

OLIVIA
It's you at last, Alex! What on earth kept you?
Where is Gay?

O'PARK
He's with me

OLIVIA
Well, what happened ? Was there an auction ? Tell me !

O'PARK
The auction was over by four o'clock
We missed the train and had to wait hours
Oh... my head is going round....

OLIVIA
You have been drinking   [Enter GAY.]
Gay ! What happened ? Tell me, for heaven's sake !

GAY
I brought some smoked salmon
I haven't had a bite to eat all day
Phew ! What an experience !

[ASHBY's loud voice, OFF.]

ASHBY
Ha ha ha ! You're snookered !

GAY
Who's that in the Billiards Room ? [EXIT.]

OLIVIA
What happened ?
Has the cherry orchard been sold ?

O'PARK
It has

OLIVIA
Who bought it ?

O'PARK
I did

OLIVIA
....
....
Oh my God in heaven!
....
.... [VERA throws the house-keys on the floor.]

O'PARK
I bought it!
Forgive me, my friends... my head is spinning!
Eh... I can't speak...
Eh... Switzer was already there when I arrived
Poor Gay had only fifteen thousand
And Switzer started the bidding at thirty... over and above the mortgage
I understood the position at once...hah
Took up the challenge...bid forty. He bid forty-five
He kept raising me by five thousand and I answered with ten
Suddenly I heard it being knocked down to me!
Now the cherry orchard is mine! Good God!
Come on: tell me I'm crazy! Tell me I'm drunk!
 [He does a little dance.]
Don't laugh at me!
If my father could only see this...rise from the grave
He thought I was stupid...lazy and stupid! Hah!
You saw me run barefoot around the estate
Winter and Summer
Well, it's the same little Alex has bought your estate
The most beautiful estate in the world!
I've bought the estate where my father and grandfather
Were little better than slaves
Where they weren't even allowed stick their noses inside the kitchen
I must be dreaming! I must be imagining it!
It can't be... it's a fantasy! A mystery! Hah!

She's thrown down the keys !
Wants to show she's no longer mistress here
Hear the music of those keys !
Hey, musicians ! Play up ! I want to hear you play !
Come on everyone
See Alex O'Park take an axe to the cherry orchard !
Root and branch ! Root and branch !
Hear them crashing down all round !
I'm going to cover the estate with spanking new houses
And our grandchildren and great-grandchildren
Will see a new life springing up here. Music !

[OLIVIA seems broken.]

Why didn't you listen ?
You poor unfortunate woman
You will never get it back now
Oh I hope it's all over and done with soon !
Our unhappy, mixed-up life somehow changed soon
Ay, what's going on ? Play up ! Let's hear that music !
Let's have everything the way I say it now !
Here comes the new landlord !
The owner of the cherry orchard !
Ooops ! Never mind: I can pay for everything !

[Exit O'PARK. Enter VERA.
Enter TIMMS, who stays at a distance.]

VERA
Mother, Mother, why are you crying ?
My dear good kind Mother... my darling Mother
The cherry orchard is sold. It is gone... that's the truth... I know it
But don't cry, Mother
You still have your life waiting for you
You've still got your gentle loving heart
Come with me, my darling
Come: away from here
We'll plant a new orchard like there's never been before
You will see it and you will know
And joy: profound, serene joy will steal into your soul

Sink into your heart like the evening sun sinking into the lake
And that will make you smile again, Mother !
Come, my darling... come !

PART FOUR

[The house has been cleared of all but the remnants of its furnishings. Bags are packed and ready to go. ASHBY has a tray with glasses of champagne. DINEEN quietly tying up a box or securing suitcases. ASHBY addresses O'PARK.]

ASHBY
The tenants have arrived *en masse* to say goodbye.
In my opinion, sir, they're a decent enough lot, but quite ignorant of course

[Enter OLIVIA and GAY who exit after saying:]

GAY
You gave them your purse, Olivia
There was no need for that
You really shouldn't have done it

OLIVIA
I... I couldn't help it. I simply couldn't help it

[O'PARK tries to stop them with:]

O'PARK
Have a glass of champagne. Please ! Just one glass
It was the last bottle they had... No ? Oh
If I'd known, I wouldn't have bought it
I don't think I'll bother...
Help yourself, Ashby

ASHBY
Thank you, sir
To those who are leaving !
And here's to you sir, who isn't
....
This isn't real champagne
You can take that from me, sir

O'PARK
Well I damn well paid enough for it
It's cold as hell in here

ASHBY
That's all right. Because we're leaving. Ha ha ha !

O'PARK
What's the joke ?

ASHBY
Nothing
I just feel happy

O'PARK
Look out there
The day is full of calm sunshine... perfect building weather
Look at the time: we don't want to miss that train.
                                              [Enter TIMMS.]
TIMMS
We don't want to miss that train
The cars are at the door
Vera, have you seen my raincoat ?

O'PARK
I have to go to Cork
I'll be on the train as far as Dublin with you
I'm exhausted hanging around here doing nothing
I can't live without work
Don't know what to do with my hands
Look... they just flop around like they belong to someone else

TIMMS
We'll soon be gone
And you can resume your valuable labours

O'PARK
Have a glass of champagne

TIMMS
No.
Thanks

O'PARK
So... back to Oxford, eh ?

TIMMS
Yes. I'll see them as far as London

O'PARK
Of course
I expect the professors have suspended lectures until you get back
All on tenderhooks for your eminent return

TIMMS
Why don't you mind your own business ?

O'PARK
How many years have you been a student now ?

TIMMS
Try coming up with something new for a change
That one is a bit stale, don't you think ?
I expect we'll never run into each other again
So let me give you a bit of advice
Stop waving your arms about
And while I'm at it; to build semi-detached houses on the expectation
That the denizens will some day become landowners
Is about as useful as that waving your arms around
There's something about you that I actually like
You have fine sensitive fingers, like an artist's
And you have a fine sensitive soul

O'PARK
My dear Peter !
Thanks for everything. Let me lend you some money. You may need it

TIMMS
Need it ? Whatever for ?

O'PARK
I bet you haven't a fiver to your name

TIMMS
Oh yes I have. I've just got paid for a translation: I have it right here
Wonder where that raincoat of mine could have got to

VERA [OFF]
Oh there's your wretched coat ! [Throws coat in.]

TIMMS
Why are you so cross, Vera ?
Hey ! This isn't my raincoat !

O'PARK
I had about three thousand acres of rape-seed this year.
What a killing !
And when they were in bloom, what a sight they made ! Beautiful !
So, you see, I can well afford to lend you some of that profit
I'd be more than glad to
Don't be stand-offish !
I'm a peasant: I'm offering you something man to man

TIMMS
Your father was a peasant, mine was a chemist
All of which means absolutely nothing
Put it away ! Put it away !
If you offered me two hundred thousand, I wouldn't accept it
I'm a free spirit
Everything you value so highly

All the things you people, rich or poor
Think give you status and self-esteem
Have no more value to me than a wisp of straw blown about in the air
I don't need you... I walk past you
I am strong and proud
Humanity is on the march towards a higher truth
Towards a Utopian dream come true
And I am in the vanguard of that march !

O'PARK
Do you think you'll get there ?

TIMMS
I will get there
Or I will show others the way and they will get there

                    [SOUND OF AN AXE being put to a tree.]

O'PARK
Well, time to go old chap !
You and I are trying to impress each other
But life goes on regardless
Sometimes, after a really long day's work
I can see things really clear
Then I too know the meaning of my life.
Have you any idea how many people in this country
Live lives of utter pointlessness ?
... ?
Well never mind
Because they are not the few who make the world go round !
                                      [Enter VERA.]

...
And Gay has got job in the bank ! Ha ha !
 He'll never stick it,,, too damn lazy

VERA
Mother asks you not to cut down the cherry orchard
Till she's gone

TIMMS
You have no idea, have you ?   [Exit.]

O'PARK
Sorry ! I'll see to it right away
Idiots !   [Exit.]

VERA
What about the old servants ?
Have they gone to the County Hospital yet ?

ASHBY
They went this morning

VERA
Your mother is in the kitchen
She wants to say goodbye to you

ASHBY
Oh, that's the last straw !   [Exit VERA.]

DINEEN
You haven't so much as looked at me all morning, Ashby
You're going away and leaving me !
                    [She tries to embrace him
                     He tries to drink champagne.]

ASHBY
Paris !
That's the last this dump will see of us !
I can't believe it ! *Vive la France !*
I hate it here ! Not at all suitable
Not at all the kind of life I want
It was inevitable, Dineen
I've had a bellyfull of this ignorance
More than a bellyfull

What's the point in weeping like that ?
Behave yourself and you won't end up in tears

DINEEN
Look at my make-up !
Write to me from Paris, Ashby, please !
I did love you... I loved you so much
I'm really full of love, Ashby !

ASHBY
They're coming !

[Enter OLIVIA, GAY and VERA.}

GAY
We're running out of time
Who's been eating pickles ?   [ASHBY ?]

OLIVIA
In ten minutes we'll be on the train
Goodbye, dear house... grandfather house !
Winter will pass and Spring will come
And you won't be here any more
They will pull you down
If these walls could talk, eh ?
Vera, my precious, you look so beautiful
And happy. Are you happy ?

VERA
A new life is beginning, Mother !

GAY
Indeed. Everything is all right finally
We were all under a great strain
Before the cherry orchard was sold
But now that it has finally happened
We are serene and, yes, happy even
I'm a bank official now... a financial consultant !
Pot the red in the middle

As for you, Olivia, say what you like
You are looking really well again. Isn't she ?

OLIVIA
My nerves are better. They are
I seem to have discovered how to sleep again
Take my things out, Ashby: it is time
I'll see you very soon, Vera love
I'll live in Paris till the money your great-aunt sent
To buy the cherry orchard runs out...
Well, three cheers for old Aunt Charlotte !

VERA
Come home soon, Mother... very soon
We'll read lots of books together
And I want to see all kinds of places with you
You will come back, won't you, Mother ?

OLIVIA
I'll come back, my lovely one !

[Exit ASHBY and DINEEN with luggage,
VERA with a box. Enter O'PARK.]

GAY
Everyone is leaving me. Vera's going away
All of a sudden I'm deserted
Alex, I have something for you. There: take it...four hundred
I still owe you eight hundred and forty
I haven't forgotten !

O'PARK
I must be dreaming ! Ha ha ha !
Where did this come from ?

GAY
Two English chaps have been hanging around

That farm of mine at Coolblaney
Some kind of special clay they're after
And there's four hundred off what I owe you, my dear
Yes., take it, take it !   There'll be more where that came from
Young chap on the train was telling me
That eh this great philosopher advises people to jump off roofs
'Jump !' he says
'That will solve all your problems'
Good heavens: can you imagine !

O'PARK
Who were these Englishmen ?

GAY
I let them have thirty acres on a long lease
It's entailed you know
Men of enormous intellect, these English chaps !
You'd better get on the road

OLIVIA
We're all ready
I have just two things on my mind
The old servants... we have five minutes, haven't we ?

GAY
They've been taken to the County Hospital
Myself and Ashby sent them off in a cab this morning
Happy as Larry.   [Exit.]

OLIVIA
The other thing is Vera
I really hoped to see her settled by this time
As you very well know, I always thought that you...
I mean, everything pointed to you two...
Getting married
She loves you... you like her
I simply do not know why the pair of you avoid the issue

I don't understand it

O'PARK
To tell you the truth, neither do I... it's very peculiar
If there's still time, I'm ready even now
Let's just do it and get it over with
If you go, I don't think I'll do it

OLIVIA
It'll only take one minute. I'll fetch her right now

O'PARK
I have the champagne and everything !
Oh it's all gone. Someone must have scoffed it !

[ASHBY clears his throat and follows OLIVIA out.]

OLIVIA
Vera, I want you. Hurry, please !

O'PARK
Aye

[Enter VERA, who will do some elaborate examination of luggage.]

VERA
I know it's not in that one...

O'PARK
What are you looking for ?

VERA
I packed it myself and...

O'PARK
Vera
....

Where are you going, Vera ?

VERA
Mullingar. Our cousin's place
I've agreed to look after their house
To be their housekeeper actually

O'PARK
So far away ?
....
And life comes to an end in this house

VERA
It must be in the trunk
Yes, life comes to an end in this house
Finally to an end

O'PARK
....
Last year we had a ferocious storm at this time
Now everything is calm and sunny
Though frost is forecast I believe

VERA
Our barometer has been stuck at 'Set Fair' for years

VOICE [OFF]
Mr O'Park !

O'PARK
Coming !   [Exit swiftly. VERA weeps silently.
                              Enter OLIVIA followed by GAY.]

OLIVIA
Well ?
....
We must go

VERA
Yes it's time, Mother dear
I don't want to miss that train

GAY
My dears... my dearest dearest dears
Leaving this house for ever
Parting from you like this
How can I remain silent
How can I not attempt to express
The emotions that engulf me....

VERA
Gay, please !

GAY
Pot the red... pot the red...mum's the word eh ?
                    [Enter TIMMS and O'PARK.]

TIMMS
Ladies, it's time

OLIVIA
I just want to sit down for one last minute
I feel as though I'm seeing this house
This room for the very first time
I see them and feel overwhelmed
By sweet anticipation

GAY
I remember like it was yesterday
Easter Sunday morning
I was six years old and I sat on that window sill
Watching my father going out to church

OLIVIA

Is everything out ?

O'PARK
I think so

OLIVIA
We shall lock the front door
And there won't be a living soul left in this house

O'PARK
In the spring I'll be back

> [VERA pulls an umbrella from a bag, with great violence. O'PARK makes a pretence of being startled.]

VERA
Good God ! You didn't really think I...

TIMMS
I can hear the train in the valley

VERA
There's your precious raincoat, Peter ! Phew !
It really is time you threw it away [But TIMMS puts it on.]

TIMMS
Now, ladies and gentlemen...

GAY
....
....
Train....
Station....
In off,,, in off...

OLIVIA

Let's go !

O'PARK
Is everyone out ?
No one left behind
....
That door should be locked
Let's go !

VERA
Goodbye this house !
Goodbye this life !

TIMMS
Hail new life !   [VERA, TIMMS exit..]

O'PARK
So, house... till Spring !
Ladies and gentlemen...   [Exit,]

[GAY and OLIVIA are left alone. As if at a signal they fling themselves, sobbing, into each other's arms.]

GAY
Oh my dear Olivia !

OLIVIA
My dear, my sweetest dear !
....
....
My beautiful orchard !
My life, my youth, my joy, goodbye !

VERA [OFF]
Ma-ma !

TIMMS [OFF]

Where are you?

OLIVIA
Coming!
Coming!

[Exeunt.
Empty stage. Door locked behind the departed.
Car doors slam, cars heard leaving.
Muffled sad sound of AXE striking a tree.
Silence. Footsteps heard. AN OLD SERVANT shuffles in and to the locked outer door. Looks around. 'No way out'.
Lies down and rests motionless.
From a distance we hear the sound like a string breaking, and slowly it dies away. Silence. The sound of an AXE striking a tree.]

END OF THE PLAY

Lightning Source UK Ltd.
Milton Keynes UK
UKOW01f1855190917
309503UK00004B/461/P